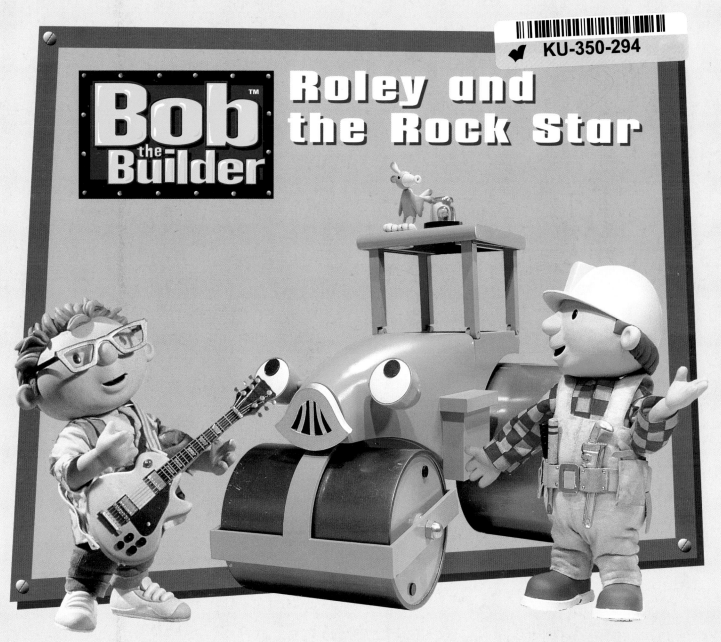

Bob the Builder™
Roley and the Rock Star

BBC

It was a very sunny morning. Bob looked at the barometer on his wall.

"Wow! It's going to be really hot today!" he said. Bob's fish, Finn, splashed the water with his tail.

"I wish I could swim around all day and keep cool like you!" laughed Bob.

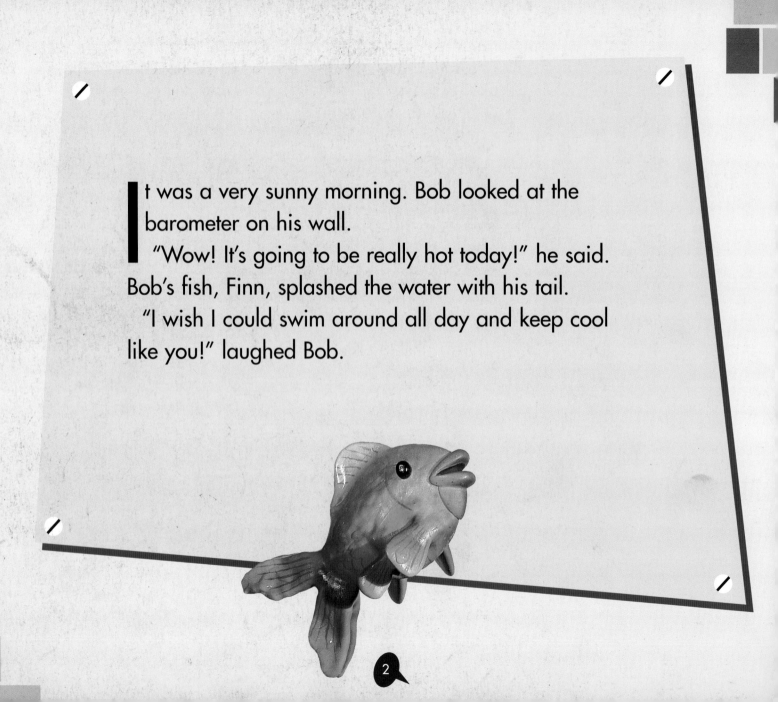

When Bob went out into the yard Wendy was loading tools into Muck's scoop.

"Morning, everyone!" said Bob.

"Morning, Bob!" Wendy and the machines replied.

"We've got two big jobs to do today," Bob told the machines. "I've got to build a pond in Mr Lazenby's front garden and Wendy's laying out a nature trail in the country park."

"Wow!" Roley rumbled. "Lennie Lazenby is the lead singer of the Lazers. They're my top band!"

"Come on then, team. Let's go!" said Bob.

When Wendy, Muck and Lofty arrived at the country park, Wendy studied her map.

"This is where the nature trail begins, so we'll need to put a signpost right here," she said, pointing at the ground.

Wendy dug a deep hole and Lofty carefully lowered the first signpost into the ground.

"What's a nature trail?" asked Muck.

"It's a path that people can follow to see all kinds of animals and plants," Wendy replied.

Further along the nature trail, Wendy and Muck were studying the map, working out where the next signpost had to go.

When they weren't looking, a little duckling popped out in front of Lofty.

"**Quack!**" it said.

"Ooooh!" Lofty wailed.

"What's the matter, Lofty?" called Wendy.

"A great big quacking thing just jumped out," he cried.

"A duck?" asked Wendy. But the duckling had hopped back into the bushes.

"I can't see any ducks. You must be dreaming, Lofty," said Muck.

Lofty kept a look-out for quacking things while Muck and Wendy built a stile over a fence.

Suddenly two little ducklings waddled in front of Lofty and Muck.

"Oooooh…er!" said Lofty as he ducked behind a bush.

"Quack! Quack!"

went the ducklings.

Then another duckling appeared on the top of Lofty's jib!

"Lofty, you were right. Hello, little duckling!" said Wendy.

"Ooooh, Wendy! Take it away," he cried.

"You silly billy, Lofty," said Wendy. "The ducklings are more frightened of you than you are of them!"

"But I won't hurt them," said Lofty.

"I know, but sometimes people are scared of things for no reason at all. I wonder why they're so far away from the pond?" said Wendy. "Come on, team, let's take them back to the water."

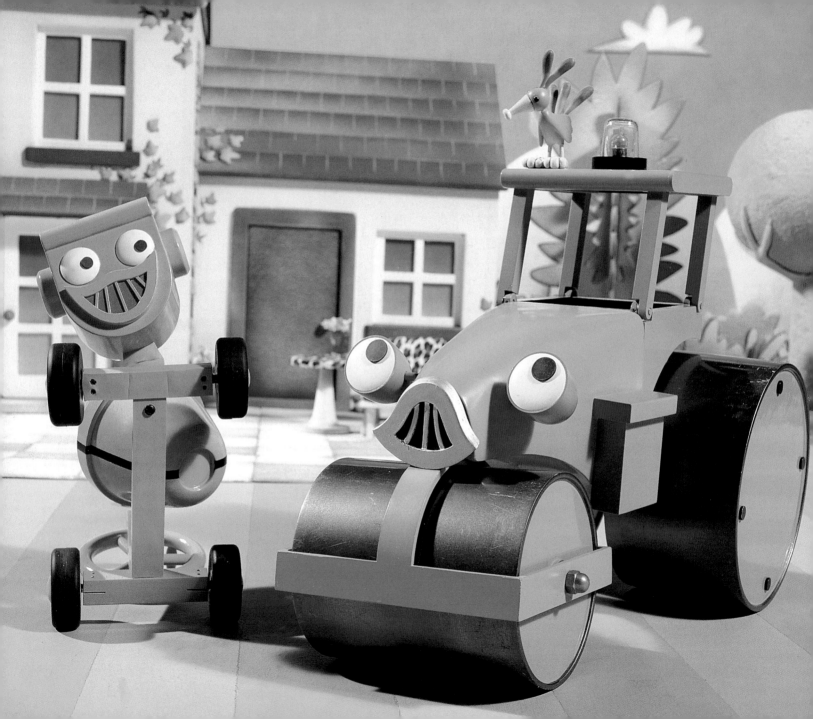

Meanwhile, at Lennie Lazenby's house, Bob, Dizzy and Roley could hear loud music.

"Ooooh, it makes me want to dance!" cried Dizzy, as she got up and started to wiggle.

"Hey, Dizzy, let's rock and roll!" cried Roley.

"Toot! Toot!" chirped Bird, as he bobbed up and down on top of Roley's cab.

While Roley and Dizzy were dancing, Scoop dug a big hole for the pond, and Bob lined it with a waterproof sheet.

"I'll need lots of cement for the rockery around the pond," Bob told Dizzy.

"Cement coming up!" giggled Dizzy.

Bob stuck the rocks around the edges of the pond with Dizzy's cement.

"We'll wait for the cement to set, then I'll add the finishing touch – a fountain!" said Bob.

Lennie Lazenby came out into the garden just as Bob was about to test the fountain.

"Hello, Mr Lazenby," said Bob.

"Hey, call me Lennie!" the rock star replied.

"Oh, er, right, Lennie," Bob replied.

"Oh, Lennie," said Roley, rushing up. "I really dig your music!"

"Cool! Maybe we should have a jam some time," said Lennie.

"Wow! That would be great," said Roley.

Bob pressed the switch on the wall and water bubbled up from the fountain.

18

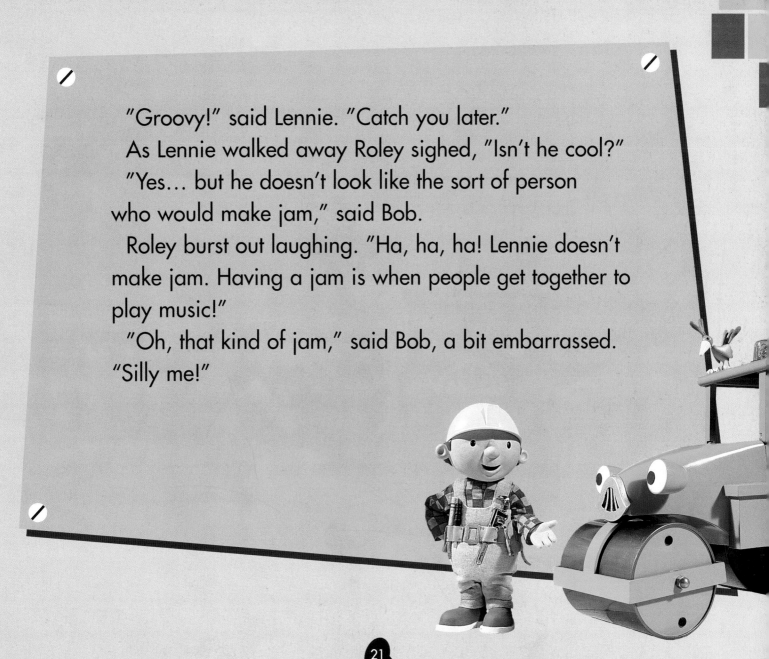

"Groovy!" said Lennie. "Catch you later."

As Lennie walked away Roley sighed, "Isn't he cool?"

"Yes... but he doesn't look like the sort of person who would make jam," said Bob.

Roley burst out laughing. "Ha, ha, ha! Lennie doesn't make jam. Having a jam is when people get together to play music!"

"Oh, that kind of jam," said Bob, a bit embarrassed. "Silly me!"

Back at the country park, Wendy had found the duck pond.

"It's been so hot lately, the pond water has all dried up," she said.

"Poor little ducklings, they must have been looking for a new home!" said Muck.

"Where's their mummy?" Lofty asked.

"I don't know, but I think we should look after the ducklings until their mother comes back," Wendy replied. "Let's see if there's room for them at the pond that Bob is building for Lennie Lazenby."

"Hi, Bob," said Wendy, when they arrived at Lennie Lazenby's house.

"Hi, Wendy," said Bob.

"**Quack! Quack!**" went the little ducklings in Muck's scoop.

"They've lost their mother and their pond in the country park has dried up," said Wendy. "Err, Mr Lazenby do you think the ducklings could stay in your pond?"

"Great idea! Ducks are, like, really groovy!" said Lennie.

25

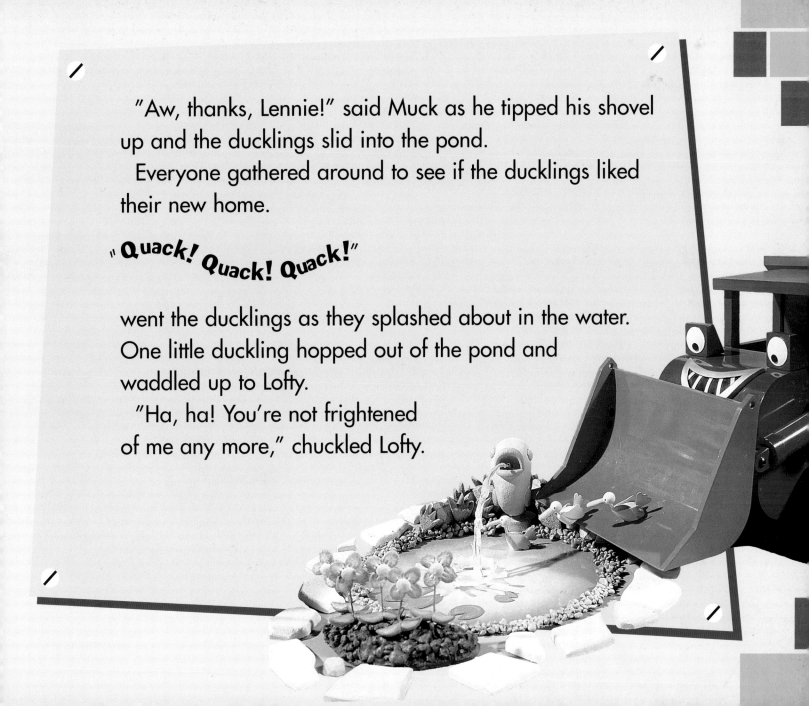

"Aw, thanks, Lennie!" said Muck as he tipped his shovel up and the ducklings slid into the pond.

Everyone gathered around to see if the ducklings liked their new home.

"**Quack! Quack! Quack!**"

went the ducklings as they splashed about in the water. One little duckling hopped out of the pond and waddled up to Lofty.

"Ha, ha! You're not frightened of me any more," chuckled Lofty.

Just then, a big duck waddled across Lennie's lawn and hopped straight into the pond. The three ducklings gathered around her.

"That's the mother duck!" cried Dizzy.

"She must have been looking for a new home and now she's found one," said Bob.

"Hey, let's celebrate!" said Lennie. "Shall I sing my new single?"

"Yes, please! That would be brilliant!" squeaked Dizzy.

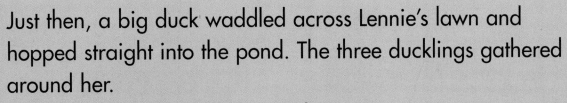

Lennie started to play his electric guitar. Bob, Wendy and all the machines danced around the garden to Lennie's music.

"**Bob the Builder, can we fix it?**" sang Bob.
"**Bob the Builder, yes, we can!**" Wendy sang back.
Soon all the machines had joined in the singing. Roley and Dizzy sang along especially loudly!

"Hey, groovy singing, Roley! Perhaps you could sing on my next album," said Lennie. "Wow! I'd love that," gasped Roley.

THE END!